COMING HOME

Contents

Written by Jean Ure

Illustrated by Joseph Roberts

Published by Pearson Education Limited, Edinburgh Gate, Harlow, Essex, CM20 2JE
Registered company number: 872828

www.pearsonschools.co.uk

Designed by Bigtop

Illustrated by Joseph Roberts

First published 2011

15 14 13 12
10 9 8 7 6 5 4 3

British Library Cataloguing in Publication Data
A catalogue record for this book is available from the British Library

ISBN 978 0 435 91519 3

Printed and bound in Malaysia (CTP-VVP)

Acknowledgements
We would like to thank the children and teachers of Bangor Central Integrated Primary School, NI; Bishop Henderson C of E Primary School, Somerset; Brookside Community Primary School, Somerset; Cheddington Combined School, Buckinghamshire; Cofton Primary School, Birmingham; Dair House Independent School, Buckinghamshire; Deal Parochial School, Kent; Newbold Riverside Primary School, Rugby and Windmill Primary School, Oxford for their invaluable help in the development and trialling of the Bug Club resources.

TWO LEFT FEET

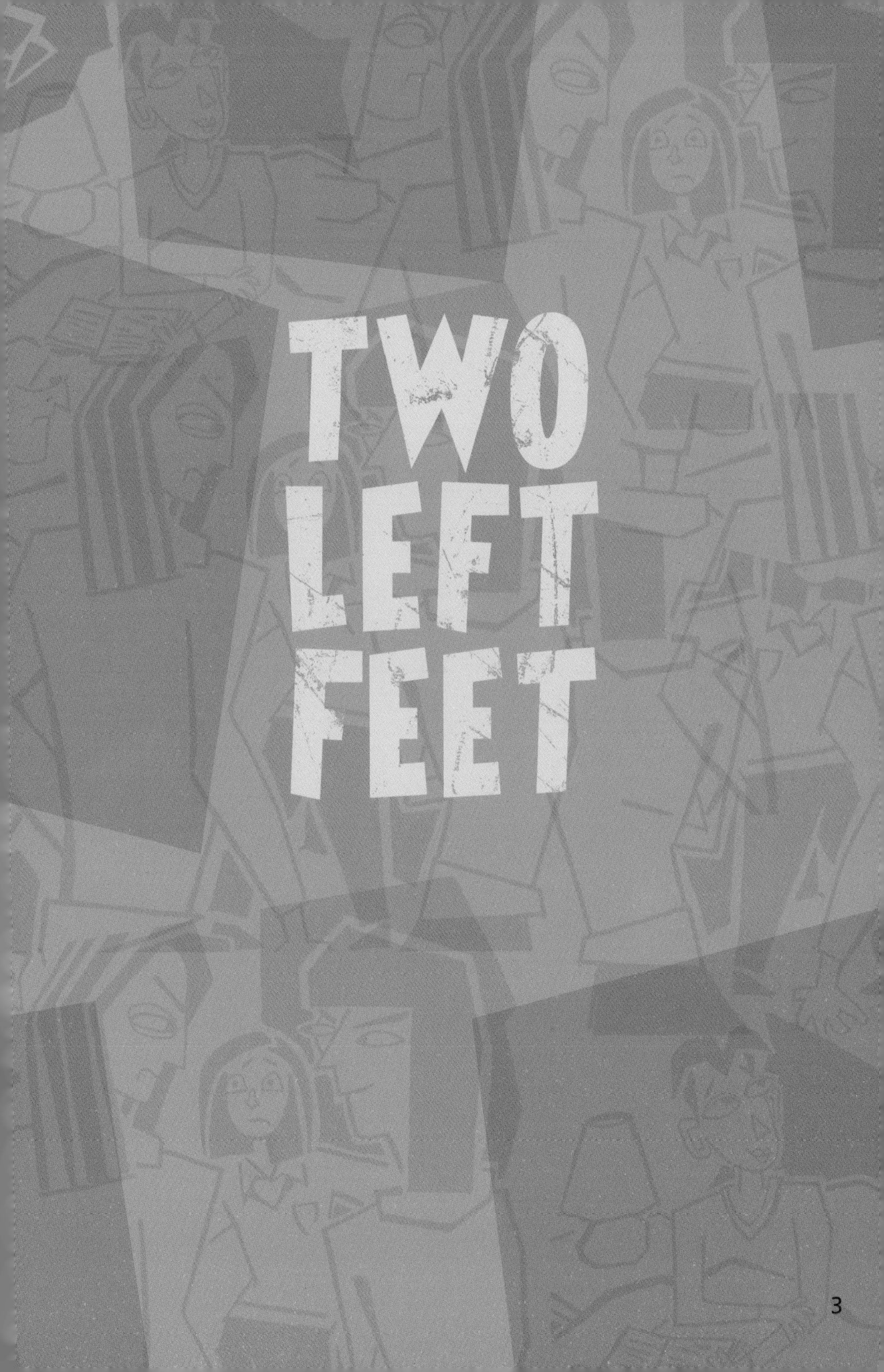

"Are you sure you don't want to do something special?" asked Mum. "After all, it is your birthday."

In two weeks' time, I was going to be twelve. Mum was really anxious that we should do something to celebrate. My sister Jodie, who is two years younger than me, always has a party. She invites loads of her friends, and they all get dressed up and giggle and shriek.

Mum knew I wouldn't want that, but she was hoping maybe I could ask some of my mates from school and we could all go up the road for a pizza, or even maybe go ten-pin bowling.

"That would be fun," she said, "wouldn't it?"

"I s'ppose so," I mumbled.

"Good!" Mum sounded pleased. "That's settled, then. I'll go ahead and arrange it. Saturday week. Ask your friends."

I did ask a couple of boys. I asked Andy Simcox 'cos he's not very popular and I thought maybe he'd say yes, and I asked Aaron Peterson 'cos he sometimes gets on the same bus. Neither of them could come. Andy said he was going to visit his nan, and Aaron – well, Aaron didn't actually say he *couldn't* come. He just gave me this odd look, like, "What's he asking me for?" and shook his head and made a kind of grunting noise.

In the end, I told Mum that I'd be quite happy just going up the road for a pizza.

"Well, it's up to you," said Mum. "I can't say it sounds like much of a birthday treat to me."

Poor Mum! I knew that she was worried about me; I'd heard her talking to Dad.

"He ought to be out enjoying himself! Not stuck indoors at that computer."

Dad said to give me a chance. "There's nothing wrong with Josh. He's just a bit shy, that's all. He'll grow out of it."

"I just want him to be happy," said Mum. "I really wish we knew more about his background."

I would like to know more about my background, too. All Mum and Dad had ever been able to tell me was that I had been found – "on a seat, in the park". I could have come from anywhere!

Jodie said maybe I was an alien. "Like from Mars, or somewhere."

I pointed out that Mars couldn't support human life, but she just giggled and said, "Whatever!"

I knew she didn't mean anything by it; she thought she was being funny. All the same, it stuck in my mind. I did sometimes wish I could be a bit more like Jodie. How come she managed to make so many friends? I'd tried really hard, but somehow it just never happened.

It would have helped if I'd been any good at football, but the truth is I was useless. Kids groaned when I was put on their team. Mr Snow, our PE teacher at primary school, used to say I had two left feet.

I'd looked at my feet most carefully and they seemed to me pretty much the same as other people's as far as I could make out, but I have this thing – I can't tell left from right. I really can't!

Someone asked me, one day, how to get to the High Street. I *knew* how to get to the High Street; I could have walked there quite easily. But I couldn't give directions! I heard myself mumbling, "You go down there, and then you kind of ... go round there, and then you ... go on a bit, and then ..." And then I gave up.

It was quite embarrassing.

It's a bit like being dyslexic, except that has a name. Lots of people are dyslexic. As far as I knew, I was the only person in the entire world who couldn't kick a football in the right direction. People would yell at me:

"Left! *Left!*"

Then I'd score an own goal and they'd all groan. Everybody got quite sick of me.

When I started at secondary school, I thought that things would be different. I would join in, and make jokes, and be just like everyone else. Only it didn't happen. Lots of the boys from primary school had moved on with me so it wasn't any use thinking I could suddenly become a different person. Already there had been a familiar scene on the football field.

"Good heavens, boy! Can't you tell left from right?"

Nothing had changed; nothing seemed likely to change. Until one day, in the middle of a Maths lesson, just three weeks into the winter term …

Is there anybody there?

What???

I sprang round. Behind me, in front of me, all over the class, people were nose down into their Maths books. Mr Daley is not someone to be messed with. As he frequently reminds us, "I have eyes in the back of my head!"

"Problem?" he asked.

"No, sir."

I sank back into my seat, squinting sideways at Aaron Peterson, and sideways in the other direction at Paul Finnegan. Both were scribbling industriously. But one of them must have spoken! I hadn't been imagining it.

Or had I?

No! I couldn't have. The thought was too scary. Resolutely, I pushed it to the back of my mind. If I just ignored it, maybe it would go away.

It didn't happen again. Not during the day. I thought I was safe. But that night, in bed, just as I was falling asleep, it started up again. Louder this time, and more insistent. Even a bit cranky.

Why don't you answer me? Say something!

What do you want? The thought had formed itself before I could stop it. I heard a chuckle. It sounded triumphant.

I knew it! Why have you taken so long to answer? I've been calling for hours!

I realised that there had been a strange, low-level buzzing in my head all afternoon. I'd been doing my best to pretend it wasn't there. I couldn't pretend any longer. My thoughts, unbidden, apologised for me.

Sorry. I couldn't hear you properly. WHO ARE YOU?

Taz. Who are you?

I'm Josh.

Suddenly, it felt quite normal to be talking to a voice that existed only in my head. A bit like an internal telephone system. I was dimly aware that to most people it would seem weird, to say the very least, but for once I wasn't bothered about other people. I was eager to talk.

Taz? You still there?

You'd better believe it! I think we might live quite close. Which school you at?

Swithin Bank. You?

St Giles.

St Giles! I knew St Giles. It was in the same town. Thoughts were forming thick and fast, tumbling over themselves in my head.

Which year?

Year 7.

Me too!

So many questions I wanted to ask. So many things I wanted to know! By the time we reluctantly closed down it was almost midnight. We'd been talking for an hour and a half! It was the longest conversation I had ever had. Before we signed off we agreed that we must get together.

Town Hall Gardens? Saturday morning? 'bout eleven?

You're on!

Next day at school I did something I had never done before: I made a joke. We were sitting in the hall, having lunch: jacket potato, sweet corn and baked beans. Aaron Peterson was stirring his beans round his plate, glaring at them like they'd done him some kind of personal injury.

"**Beans!**"

He spat the word out, in a torrent of loathing. That was when I got inspired. I picked up a bean and tossed it into the middle of the table.

"What's that?"

Everyone leaned forward. "It's a *bean*," said Aaron.

"So what's this?" I squashed it – splat! – with the handle of my knife. "What's it now?"

"Squashed bean," said Aaron.

"*Has*-bean!" I snatched up another one. "Now it's a bean ... now it's a has-bean!"

"Oh. Yeah! I get it. That's not bad," said Aaron. He leaned across the table and smashed a bean in front of me. Within seconds, everyone was at it. "Now it's a bean ... now it's a has-bean!"

"Way to go!" cried Aaron.

For the first time, I felt that I was accepted. I'd made a joke. I was one of them!

The following day was Saturday.

"I'm going out," I told Mum. "Going to meet a friend."

Mum said, "That's nice! Who is he? Someone from school?"

It was Jodie who saved me.

"Could be a she," she said, giving me this sly glance. "Have you got a girlfriend?"

"Wouldn't tell you if I had," I said, and made my escape.

At eleven o'clock on a Saturday morning, the Town Hall Gardens were full of people. I hesitated. *Taz?*

Across the grass, a boy was waving. Just an ordinary-looking boy, same as me. Nothing weird about him. No pointy ears, no antenna growing out of his head. Just a boy. I waved back and went rushing over.

Yay!

We exploded in silent triumph, our hands meeting in a high five. A woman walking past with a dog looked at us, curiously.

Hastily, we exchanged thoughts.

Talk normally?

Probably best.

We went round those gardens four times, talking non-stop. Having to say words out loud now seemed a bit of a slow and clumsy method of communicating, but we knew we shouldn't draw attention to ourselves. I confessed that my sister already thought I was weird.

"She said the other day she thought I was an alien."

"Yeah," Taz nodded. "I know what you mean. My gran once said she thought I must have dropped by from another planet. She reckons I'm a one-off."

"I was adopted," I said.

"Me too," said Taz.

"I don't know anything about my real parents."

"I don't know anything about mine. I was found."

"So was I! I was found in a park."

"I was found in the woods."

There was a moment of silence, as we both thought about it.

"Don't suppose it was anywhere near here?" I asked.

"Chorlton Woods. How about you?"

"Abbey Park."

Within a stone's throw ...

"You don't think – " I hesitated. "You don't think we could be twins?"

We didn't look much alike, but then twins don't necessarily have to.

"I guess it would account for the – " Taz waved a hand. "You know! The thing up here." He tapped his head.

"Telepathy," I said. "It's what happens with twins."

A ball came towards us with a dog in hot pursuit. I kicked it for him – in totally the wrong direction.

"Hey!" Taz sounded excited. "I do that!"

"Do what?" I said, not quite sure I wanted to admit, even to Taz, that I couldn't kick a ball properly.

"Do what you just did." He aimed a swipe at an imaginary ball. "You didn't mean to kick it over there, did you?" He grinned. "Got two left feet?"

I grinned back. "Can't tell left from right?"

"Yeah!" Taz punched the air, exultantly. "Happens all the time!"

It was an amazing moment.

We agreed, as we parted company, that we would meet again next Saturday. We also agreed that we would continue with our silent chats, but only once a day, and only for short periods.

"Don't want to wear things out," said Taz.

We needn't have worried. If anything, our powers started to grow stronger. During that week, other voices began breaking through, wanting to introduce themselves, wanting to talk. Taz and I discussed it excitedly when we met. Counting up, we discovered that so far, between us, we'd heard from eight others. Five boys and three girls. All of us able to understand each other, even when we spoke different languages. And all of us exactly the same age.

There was a pause. I wondered if Taz were thinking what I was thinking. We couldn't all be twins ...

I was puzzling over it late that night when quite suddenly, without any warning, it was like a door in my head had burst open and let in a whole new world of excited chatter. Voices came crowding from all over, eager to make contact. To begin with it was total confusion. I couldn't even get through to Taz for all the buzzing and swarming that was going on.

Pretty quickly I learned how to filter, and managed to find Taz amongst all the babble. Taz said that he was having the same experience.

How many d'you reckon there are?

I reckoned at least a hundred. *Maybe more.*

There was a pause. Then we both thought together: *WHO ARE WE?*

That was the big question, the one we were all starting to ask. Only nobody seemed to have the answer.

And then, out of the blue, it happened. I was sitting in the kitchen with Mum and Jodie, having tea. I was about to cram a piece of cake in my mouth when – **BAM!** An arrow of light shot across my brain.

Mum said, "Josh?"

But I'd already pushed back my chair and was gone, racing up the stairs, two at a time, to my room. Instead of the usual screen saver, a message was flashing at me from the computer.

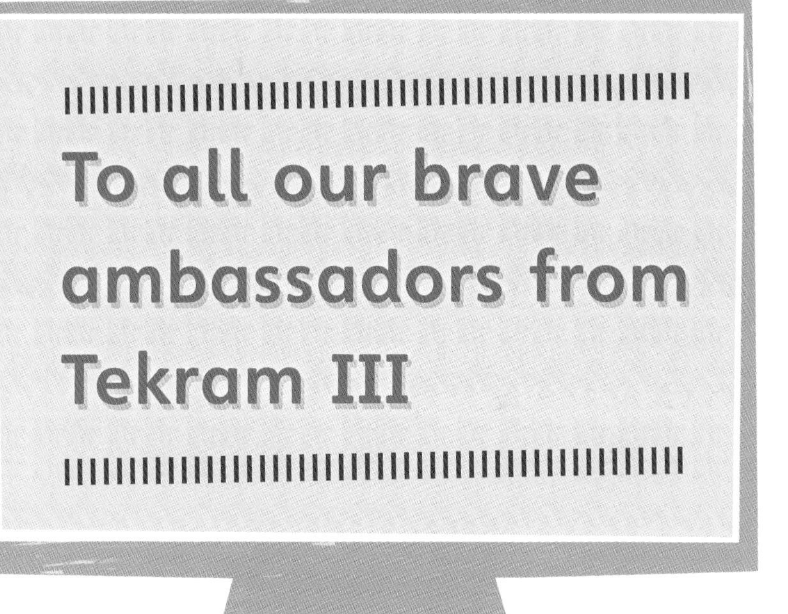

I didn't stop to wonder how it had got there. I just had this incredible feeling that after a long, long time I had come home.

Greetings from Tekram III

The hour has come for us to break our silence. By now your senses will be fully awakened, and you will be talking amongst yourselves, asking questions, seeking answers. We prepared this communication in advance, to be accessed as soon as you reached the right stage of development.

Millennia ago, as we on Tekram reckon time – just twelve short years, as you will have learned to reckon it on Earth – vast fleets of pods containing thousands of precious young seedlings were despatched to all corners of the galaxy, in the hope that at least some of them would find a resting place, where they could mature and thrive, and make a life for themselves.

Earth, although a young and unstable planet, was nonetheless judged to be one of the most promising locations.

Its inhabitants were still immature and distressingly prone to violence, but we had observed a basic level of humanity. This gave us hope that they would welcome our emerging seedlings into their midst and cherish them as their own. We very much trust that this has been the case.

By the time this message reaches you, Tekram will long since have ceased to exist. The planet was in its death throes even as we launched you on your journey. Do not mourn for us; all life cycles must come to an end.

We wish you well, our children! Strive always to be a credit to your original home, and use every endeavour to bring peace to your new one.

We salute you!

"Josh?"

That was Jodie, battering at the door. Already, the message was starting to fade.

"Mum wants to know if you're going to finish your tea."

Reluctantly, I tore myself away and followed her back downstairs. As I sat down again at the kitchen table, Taz burst excitedly into my head.

Man! You just read what I just read?

From the clamour going on, it seemed that we'd all been reading it. Firmly, I shut out everyone except Taz.

Yeah, I just read it.

Man, that explains everything. We need to talk!

Both Mum and Jodie were looking at me.

Gotta go, I told Taz. *Speak in a minute.*

"Everything OK?" asked Mum.

"Fine," I said.

I was cramming food into my mouth and swallowing it as fast as I could. I couldn't wait to get back upstairs and call Taz!

"In a rush," I said. "Someone I gotta speak to."

"Your friend?" asked Mum, brightly. "The one you went to meet? What's his name?"

"Taz," I said. Then, carelessly, I added, "He's an alien."

There was a silence.

"Well, that's nice," said Mum.

Jodie giggled. "That makes two of you!"

"Not just two," I said. "Could be hundreds of us. Could be thousands." I gulped down the last of my orange juice. "Have to go now. Got stuff to talk about."

"Alien stuff, I s'ppose."

"That's right," I said. "Alien stuff."

Jodie could tease me all she liked. So what if I had two left feet? I was proud of who I was!

A VERY SPECIAL GIFT

"Left, Josh! Left! To me, to me … left, left, left!"

They roared it at me as I raced up the field.

"LEFT, LEFT, LEFT!"

I aimed a mighty swipe.

"Way to go!"

Jason Murray thumped me on the back. A couple of other players threw their arms round me. A cheer rang out.

My own team just groaned. I'd gone and done it again … passed the ball straight to a member of the other side.

People were used to it by now. Josh Harper and his two left feet! I used to think I was the only person in the entire world who couldn't kick a football in the right direction. Then I'd discovered the Others. I wasn't alone any more. There were hundreds of us, maybe even thousands, and none of us could tell left from right. We all had two left feet!

At the end of the game I rushed to change and get upstairs for Maths with Mr Daley. He's really fierce. Just two seconds late and he'll put you in the book. For some reason I'd always felt he was harder on me than on anyone else. He always seemed to be watching, waiting for me to do something wrong.

I slid into a seat at the back, as far away as I could get from his piercing glare. He was already huffing and puffing, stabbing numbers all over the board. I sat up very straight, and concentrated, ready for when he turned round.

It was while I was concentrating that Maya came bouncing into my brain. She arrived with a great whoosh, the way she always did, taking you by surprise so you didn't have time to blot her out.

Hey, you guys!

I shook my head, impatiently. How many times had we told her? *Not while we're at school.*

As usual, she took no notice.

I'm bored! What are you both up to?

I gritted my teeth. Maya giggled. The sound went gurgling round my head like a load of soap bubbles.

Maya, GO AWAY! That was Taz, making his displeasure felt.

Maya let loose another stream of giggles. *You in class?*

Maths, I answered automatically, before I could stop myself. *I'm trying to concentrate.*

I'm in Geography, trilled Maya. *I hate Geography!*

Taz said, *Maya, I'm warning you.*

Why? Now she was defiant. *Why can't I talk? Who's to know? I can talk as much as I like. She gurgled again. Nobody can hear me!*

I heard an irritable sigh from Taz. And then a voice in my head said: JOSH?

I jerked round, startled. Who was that? That wasn't Taz!

"Ah!" Mr Daley turned from the board. "The sleeper awakes. I was wondering when we might have the pleasure of your company."

I mumbled, "Sorry, sir, I wasn't asleep, sir, I was concentrating, sir."

"But on what?" asked Mr Daley. He gave me this searching look, like he really wanted to know. Someone sniggered, and I felt myself grow red. Why did Mr Daley always seem to pick on me?

I was careful to pay full attention for the remainder of the lesson, but after Maths we had History with Mr Kent, who lives in a world of his own, which means you can take things a bit easy. I wondered again about the strange voice. Voices in the head don't sound the same as voices out loud, but you do quite quickly learn to recognise them. This definitely wasn't one of the Others.

There's a little cluster of us that live in the same area. Me and Taz and Maya actually live in the same town, though we go to different schools. We don't have any trouble communicating – we all come through loud and clear.

The rest of us are scattered, not just in this country but all over the world. You can tell when someone's a long way off; their voices tend to come and go. The voice that said "Josh" had been strong and powerful – and it hadn't sounded like a twelve-year-old. But that was what we were: just twelve years old. All of us. How could there be anyone older?

I discussed it with Taz, later that night. We usually have a chat before we go to sleep. Sometimes with Maya, sometimes just the two of us. Tonight it was just the two of us, and I was glad about that. Maya, with her reckless chatter, was making me nervous. She'd already told us how some of the girls in her class were beginning to gang up on her. They'd obviously seen her pulling faces and giggling as she chatted to me and Taz. Maybe she was braver than we were, but it just seemed to me like asking for trouble.

Taz agreed. *We'll have another go at her. Tell me more about this voice.* I told Taz how strong it had been. How it had sounded older than the rest of us.

Taz was as puzzled as I was. How could there be anyone older? We'd all arrived on Earth together, as seedlings!

We decided we'd just have to wait and see if it happened again. And if it did, should I answer or should I pretend not to have heard? The mystery voice was a bit of a worry.

We told Maya about it when we met up in the shopping centre on Saturday morning. Needless to say, she couldn't see what the problem was.

But that's exciting! Her voice squealed exultantly round my head. *To think there might be more of us, just waiting to communicate!*

She clapped her hands and laughed, and a couple of girls passing by glanced at her, curiously.

"Talk out loud," I said.

"Oh. Pooh!" Maya did a little twirl. "Why should I?"

"'Cos we don't want to draw attention to ourselves."

"Why not?" Maya tossed her head. "I'm not ashamed of who I am!"

"I'm not ashamed, either," I said. "I just don't want to upset people."

"Why should they be upset? Just 'cos we can do something they can't! Why try to hide it?"

I'd done a lot of thinking about that, myself. I had been ashamed, once. I'd known that I was different, but I hadn't known how. That was before we'd all found one another. Before we started to talk. Then the message had come through, bursting upon us from light years away, and we'd discovered the truth. We weren't from this world at all but from a far-distant planet, Tekram III, that had disappeared millennia ago. We'd been evacuated to Earth as tiny seedlings. We'd hatched here, and we'd been adopted by kind Earthlings who thought we were just ordinary babies that had been abandoned.

"Thing is," said Taz, "people don't like it when you do stuff that looks odd. It can make 'em lash out."

Maya snorted. "Just let them try!"

"It's because they're scared," I said. "It makes them feel threatened. You wouldn't want your mum and dad feeling scared, would you?"

Maya chewed at a fingernail. "S'ppose not."

"So could you please be more careful?" begged Taz.

"Yeah, 'cos I've got this teacher," I said. "He's got eyes in the back of his head and he's really got it in for me. Every time you start shrieking, I stop concentrating, and then he has a right go."

"I don't shriek," muttered Maya. But we'd obviously got through to her. I think it was the idea of her mum and dad being scared. She promised that from now on she would do her best to obey the rules. No contact while we were at school unless it was an emergency.

For the next few days, everything was quiet. The voice was quiet. Even Maya was quiet. I still had this feeling, though, that someone – or something – was out there. It was like this constant prickle in some shadowy corner of my mind. Almost as if we were being spied on.

I discussed it at night, with Taz and Maya. *It's just always there, you know?*

Maya urged me to try talking to it. *Ask what it wants. It could just want to be friends.*

I said, *Yeah, and it could be some unknown power trying to take over.*

Best just let it alone, said Taz.

Maya gave a derisive hoot. *You are so wimps, the pair of you!*

Were we wimps? Or were we just being sensible? Maya didn't know what sensible was. She had always been bold. It had never bothered her, not being able to tell left from right. She hadn't cared that she was different from other people. I sort of admired her for it, but at the same time I worried that one day she would go too far. That tough gang of girls at her school were not the sort you messed with.

At least she seemed to be keeping to her promise not to make contact during school hours. I was just starting to relax when – **WHAM!** She came barrelling into my head with such force I almost went rocketing backwards on my chair. Fortunately it was lunch time and the only teachers were at the far end of the hall.

Aaron Peterson, who was sitting opposite, looked at me in surprise.

"Found something nasty in the curry?"

I said no, I'd just swallowed the wrong way. My mind was in turmoil. Nothing but noise and confusion, and, above it all, the sound of Maya's voice, crying out.

I sat there, tense, clutching the edge of the table. Maya was obviously in some kind of trouble. Over the chaos, Taz shouted at me. *What's happening? Where is she?*

We yelled, together: *MAYA! Where are you?*

Suddenly, inside my head, there flashed an image: Maya, backed into a corner by a gang of girls. But where? Where was she? And then it came to me: the school grounds! She had to be somewhere in her school grounds.

I shoved back my chair and hotfooted it out of the hall. I could sense, in my head, that Taz was also racing to the rescue. I could hear his breathing and the thud of his feet on tarmac.

I was through the school gates and plunging down the road when a voice rang out inside my head: JOSH! TAZ! STAY WHERE YOU ARE.

I skidded to a halt, sensing Taz do the same.

GET BACK IN SCHOOL, THE PAIR OF YOU! I'VE ALREADY TAKEN CARE OF THINGS.

I hesitated.

JOSH, DON'T ARGUE WITH ME! WHAT GOOD DO YOU THINK YOU CAN DO? YOU'D NEVER GET THERE IN TIME.

It was true. Maya's school is way over the other side of town. Reluctantly, I turned back. The noise in my head was dying down. Maya had fallen silent. I tried desperately to get through to her.

Maya, say something!

Taz joined in. *Are you OK?*

She didn't answer.

Then the voice spoke again. No longer barking, but almost gentle.

Go finish your lunch. There's nothing to worry about.

I trailed back through the school gates. A teacher stood watching me. It was Mr Daley. I braced myself, waiting for him to start yelling, but to my surprise he just looked at me, frowned, and held the door.

"In you go."

Thankfully, I scuttled off. As I did so, Taz whispered in my head: *I heard it ... the voice!*

We were both too shaken to talk. We had a short, urgent exchange about Maya – why had she gone quiet? What had happened? – then lapsed into silence.

Maya got through to us later that evening. She sounded subdued, though she tried to tough it out.

I guess you were right ... I got up people's noses.

She said that one of the girls had lured her into the woods at the back of the school, where a gang of them had been lying in wait. She thought someone must have seen them, or heard them, because shortly after she'd put through her distress call to me and Taz, a couple of teachers had turned up.

We were going to come, I said. *It was just –*

The voice, said Taz.

The voice? That perked her up. *You heard it! What did it say?*

We told her as much as we could remember.

You'd have heard it yourself if you hadn't been making such a racket, said Taz.

I was being ATTACKED! said Maya. *Oh, I do hope we hear it again! There are so many things I want to ask!*

On Friday, there was a headline on the front page of the local newspaper:

MYSTERY CALLER SAVES GIRL TAUNTED BY GANG

"So now we know!" We were hanging around, the three of us, in our usual spot in the shopping centre on Saturday morning. Maya was back to being her usual bouncy self. There was a note of triumph in her voice. "I told you it didn't mean any harm!"

I said, "Yeah, but we still don't – " I stopped.

"What's the matter?" asked Taz.

"Teacher," I muttered.

Mr Daley. Still some way off, but he'd obviously seen us. He turned, in our direction. My heart sank. Now what?

JOSH – TAZ – MAYA!

The familiar voice barked in my head. I felt Taz stiffen and Maya suck in her breath. Whoever it was, it had proved itself friendly, but where was it coming from?

I hoped I'd find you here.

MR DALEY??? My head jerked up in disbelief. We waited in stunned silence as he came towards us.

"I'm sorry." He stopped and smiled. "Don't be scared! I'm one of you."

Maya flashed an I-told-you-so. *Pair of wimps!* Taz and I remained more cautious. Suppose it was a trap?

"I know, I know." Mr Daley nodded, sympathetically. "You're asking yourselves, how can that be? It's really quite simple. Let me explain. Some forty or so years before you arrived on Earth I was sent here as a seedling, just like yourselves.

I was part of an expedition which failed. It seems there must have been some sort of disaster when the pods entered Earth's atmosphere, as almost none of us survived. I know of only a handful of others on the whole of the planet. As a result, our abilities have never developed as they should. Yours are so much stronger! And, I suspect, they will continue to grow. Which is why it's only sensible, while you're young, to be discreet."

I could feel Maya blushing.

"I know it's a temptation to have fun, and there's no reason you shouldn't. But please, I'm asking you … no showing off! Such powers can do an enormous amount of good in the world – or an enormous amount of harm. It's up to you to use them for the benefit of these people who have made us so welcome. Always remember, you have a VERY SPECIAL GIFT."

He paused to let his words sink in.

"We'll speak again later. I'm sure

you must have lots of questions. In the meantime, Josh, I'll see you on Monday. Don't forget your Maths homework!"

Mr Daley walked on, leaving the three of us somewhat dazed. Even Maya, for the moment, had been silenced. I found it hard to believe that just a few months ago I'd been worried that I was weird and different. Now here I was with a very special gift!

Taz picked up on my thoughts. “I guess – ” he raised his foot to kick at an empty drinks can – “I guess we shouldn’t get too big-headed.”

“I guess we shouldn’t kick that can,” said Maya.

Too late! Taz had already kicked it. We watched, in silent dismay, as it flew off in the wrong direction across the shopping centre and into a crowd of shoppers.

“Big-headed?” said Maya. She cackled. “I don’t think so!”

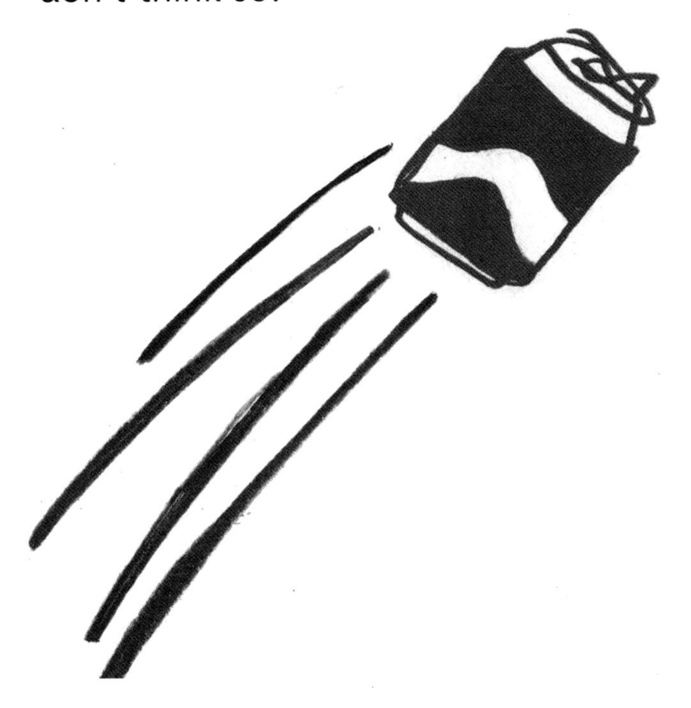